D1416428

Ella and One Great Race

LaunchCrate Publishing
Kansas City, KS

C. L. Fails

Ella and One Great Race
Written and Illustrated by: C. L. Fails

© 2019 LaunchCrate Publishing

LaunchCrate Publishing
Kansas City, KS
info@launchcrate.com
www.launchcrate.com

Ordering Information:
Quantity sales. Special discounts are available on quantity purchases by corporations, associations, and others. For details, contact the publisher at the email address above. Orders by U.S. trade bookstores and wholesalers.

Library of Congress Control Number: 2019916119

ISBN:978-1-947506-14-5

Printed in the United States of America
10 9 8 7 6 5 4 3 2 1

First Edition

The race is only as great as you make it!

"You can do this. You don't know the meaning of can't,"
Ella heard in her mind as she gazed at an ant.
Today she would race as she'd practiced for,
even though her stomach had bubbles galore.

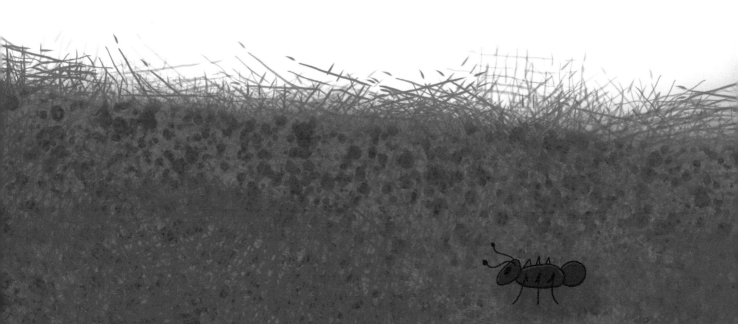

Her breathing sped up as she stood there waiting.
They all looked so ready. Her heart was pulsating.
Ga-Lump, GA-LUMP, her little heart thumped.
So nervous and anxious, so eager and pumped.

The starting bell sounded and off they went!
People ran like the race was a 40-yard sprint.
Her little legs couldn't move that fast,
and as hard as she tried, she just kept getting passed.

Ella's frustration showed on her face.
She couldn't keep up with their furious pace.
Her eyebrows did furrow, her shoulders they slumped.
Her courage, it seemed, had hit a speed bump.

Then right as mom was about to speak up,
she saw young Ella take a sip from her cup.
In one deep breath she started to chant...

Her words set the pace at which Ella would run.
Mom trotted beside her and chanted for fun.
"You can do this. You don't know the meaning of can't."
Other runners joined in, and a wave had begun.

From behind them they heard a faint sound of refrain.
Ella blamed that sweet sound on her fanciful brain.
Then they heard it again from a pack in the back.

"You can do this. You don't know the meaning of can't!"

Their chant made Ella burst with glee.
"They're singing the chant that you made up for me!"
Her legs churned as fast as a train could roll.
Not really, but you should have seen her go.

The finish line was within her sight.
She was tired but yet her legs somehow felt light.
She dug deep again for one final push,
and the chant became louder with each step she took.

"You can do this. You don't know the meaning of can't."

"YOU CAN do this. You Don't Know the meaning of Can't."

"YOU CAN DO THIS. You Don't Know the Meaning of CAN'T."

"YOU CAN DO THIS. YOU DON'T KNOW THE MEANING OF CAN'T!"

The crowd at the finish line smiled and cried,
so proud at the sight of the runners they spied.
The tallest and smallest, gave all of their heart.
No matter their place, they had won from the start.

Ella's legs just churned and churned.
With each step a bit closer, a medal she'd earn.
Then crossing the line, a smile beamed from her face.
Her fists pumping the air, she had finished the race!

About the Author

C.L. Fails is the author and illustrator of the Ella Book Series, The Christmas Cookie Book Series, the Raine the Brain Series, and a slew of other unpublished short stories. She is also an educator, having served pre-school through college students in her hometown of Kansas City. When she's not working on a book, you can find her doodling on whatever object may be nearby.

Check her out: www.clfails.com

CPSIA information can be obtained
at www.ICGtesting.com
Printed in the USA
LVHW071305031219
639278LV00011B/146/P